WELCOME TO

Beast Quest

Collect the special coins in this book.
You will earn one gold coin for
every chapter you read.

Once you have finished all the chapters,
find out what to do with your gold coins at
the back of the book.

With special thanks to Tabitha Jones

www.beastquest.co.uk

ORCHARD BOOKS

First published in Great Britain in 2020 by The Watts Publishing Group

1 3 5 7 9 10 8 6 4 2

Text © 2020 Beast Quest Limited
Cover and inside illustrations by Dynamo
© Beast Quest Limited 2020

Beast Quest is a registered trademark of Beast Quest Limited
Series created by Beast Quest Limited, London

A CIP catalogue record for this book is available from the British Library.

ISBN 978 1 40836 135 1

Printed in Great Britain

The paper and board used in this book are made from wood from responsible sources

Orchard Books
An imprint of Hachette Children's Group
Part of The Watts Publishing Group Limited
Carmelite House, 50 Victoria Embankment, London EC4Y 0DZ

An Hachette UK Company
www.hachette.co.uk
www.hachettechildrens.co.uk

ARKANO
THE STONE CRAWLER

BY ADAM BLADE

ORCHARD

THE ICY F

THE NORTHERN
MOUNTAINS

THE

WESTERN OCEAN

THE FOREST
OF FEAR

THE

CONTENTS

STORY ONE

The jolting of the cart makes my bones rattle, but that's not the worst thing. I can't stop the shivers that run up and down my spine each time I think of the cargo behind me. A huge monster, terrifying and deadly, teeth thicker than my arm.

As our cart rounds a corner, the morning sun glints off tall spires and towers in the distance – here at last is the City, and King Hugo's palace. The sight makes me think of all the tales Mother told me of the brave Masters of the Beasts that have lived there through the ages. But I can't feel excited today – I am cold and sick. I've always wanted to visit the palace – but not like this, not to bring death and destruction to innocent people. I want to go home! I'd give anything just to sit by the fire, or even help with the chores. But it's too late to turn back now.

Jamil, of Hartsbridge

BIRTHDAY PARTY

A fresh breeze cooled Elenna's face as she and Tom carried yet another section of fencing across the tournament field. Her muscles ached from the hard work, but her heart felt light as they passed people setting out tiered benches, and others hanging pennants for Prince Thomas's first birthday party the next day. Nearby, Daltec, Aduro and King

Hugo were overseeing the construction of the royal seating area. The workers chatted happily, their voices mingled with the sound of hammering and sawing.

"How about giving us a hand with your magic?" Tom called as they passed Daltec.

The young wizard shrugged, then waved a hand towards them. Elenna grinned as the wooden panel in her hands became weightless then rose into the air. She watched as Daltec manoeuvred it into place as if he were conducting a band, setting it down at the end of a long fence that separated two grass runs.

"Thanks!" Tom said. "That's the jousting ground finished!"

"Have you decided if you're going to enter the jousting competition?" Elenna asked as they joined the others near the half-finished platform.

"Not this time," Tom said. "The knights will put on a great show. I'm more interested in the feasting!"

Elenna spotted Queen Aroha striding towards them across the field, smiling as she took in the preparations, her long hair blowing in the breeze. King Hugo came across to join her as she approached.

Elenna turned to bow. "Your Majesties."

"How's everything going?" Aroha asked as she reached them.

"The archery targets are up," Tom said. "And, thanks to Daltec, the jousting list is finished. We've only really got the seating still to work on. And the royal dais."

"You know, I've never actually jousted before," Queen Aroha said, gazing at the long fence separating the runs. "I'd quite like to try it. We have a similar tradition in Tangala, where we throw spears from horseback into targets."

"Isn't that rather difficult?" Hugo asked.

"I suppose, if you're not used to it,"

Aroha said. Shaking back her hair, she turned and picked a blue-and-gold lance from the nearby stand. Then she lifted it to shoulder height, narrowed her eyes, and hurled it straight across the field. It thudded into the centre of an archery target. A servant nearby looked up in shock, and Aroha gave a friendly wave.

"Wow!" Elenna said. She knew the kind of strength and skill needed to fire an arrow that distance – the queen must have muscles of iron.

"Amazing!" Hugo told his wife. "Maybe we should include that sport at the tournament for Thomas's next birthday."

"Hmm, maybe," Aroha said distractedly, frowning as she scanned the field. "Speaking of Thomas, where is he? I thought you were watching him."

Hugo's eyes widened, and he stared around as if expecting to see the toddler right in front of him. "He was just here a moment ago!" the king said.

Elenna's chest tightened with worry as she glanced about, taking in lances, hammers and heavy wooden stakes…

"Thomas!" Hugo called. "Where are you? Come to Papa!"

"Thomas!" Aroha cried. "Thomas!"

Hearing a note of panic in the queen's voice, Elenna was about to set off in search of the child. But then she spotted Captain Harkman striding towards them, a red-faced baby prince struggling in his arms.

"Thank goodness!" Aroha said.

"I found him over by the horses," Harkman told her as he drew close.

"He's always disappearing off at the moment," said King Hugo. "We need eyes in the backs of our heads!"

"Down!" Thomas squealed, still twisting and wriggling. As the captain shifted his grip, Thomas took the chance to sink his teeth into Harkman's hand.

"Ow!" Captain Harkman thrust the toddler into Aroha's outstretched arms and rubbed his hand. "Seems like there's a new fearsome Beast in Avantia!" he said, wincing.

"Thomas, that's not kind!" the queen told the child, though she was doing a poor job of hiding her smile.

Elenna heard a clatter of racing hooves and turned in alarm, just as a loud voice cut through the sounds of construction. "Stop! I order you to stop at once!" Two guards were racing towards a cart drawn by a stocky draught horse. A broad, dark-haired man with a neatly clipped beard sat in the driver's seat, a small, pale boy at his side. As the guards reached the cart, one jumped in front of it while the other reached for the horse's bridle.

"Mind out of my way!" shouted the dark-haired man. "I'm here to see the king!" He lifted his whip and lashed the horse, making it leap forward. The two guards dived aside, narrowly avoiding the animal's hooves.

"Stop at once, on pain of death!"
Captain Harkman cried, storming
across the field, sword drawn. Elenna
took her bow from her back and
hurried after Harkman with Tom at
her side. Scowling, the man on the
cart tugged at the reins, drawing his
horse to a halt.

"What is the meaning of this?"
Captain Harkman demanded.

The man got to his feet. "I've got
something very special to show His
Majesty," he said. Elenna fitted an
arrow to her bow and Tom drew his
sword as the man turned to the bulky
load in the cart and started untying
the rope holding its cover in place. "I
bring a Beast!"

Elenna gasped as a massive, claw-

like foot slid from under the cover
– its single sharp talon as long as
Elenna's arm. She aimed an arrow at
the man's chest as Tom leapt towards
the deadly cargo, sword raised.

"Don't move a muscle!" she said.

1

AN UNLIKELY STORY

Tom's grip was firm on the sword hilt, but the dark-haired man on the cart grinned.

"No need to be afraid!" said the stranger, pulling the cover back from his cart. Beneath, Tom saw a hollow eye socket and the long teeth of some kind of Beast. He stepped back, letting his sword fall to his side as

Elenna lowered her arrow. There were no eyes in the sockets, and no flesh on the blackened skull. *It's just a skeleton!*

"I, Sanek, have already slain this Beast," the man went on. "That's why I'm here – to claim my reward!"

Tom sheathed his sword as Sanek tugged the white sheet from the rest of his load, uncovering a jumble of huge, charred bones. Many of the workers in the field had downed their tools to watch. They let out a chorus of *ooh*s and *ahh*s. Daltec and Aduro quickly joined Tom and Elenna by the cart, along with Hugo and the queen. In Aroha's arms, baby Thomas stared at the skeleton, his eyes as round as marbles.

"Jamil!" Sanek said, making the

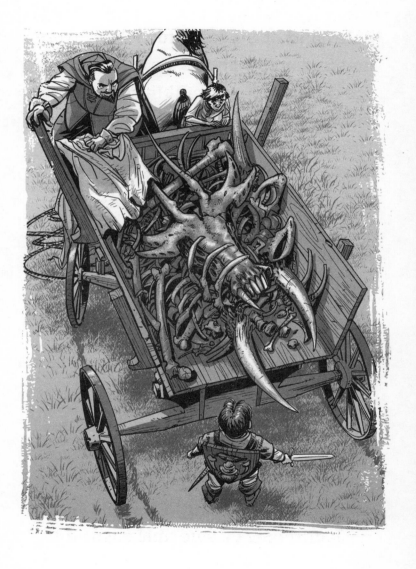

pale child at his side flinch. "Go and find water and lodging for our horse. I have important business to discuss with the king." Without a word, the lad hopped down and began unhitching their animal.

"So, tell me," Harkman demanded, addressing Sanek, as the boy led the horse away. "How did you come by your unusual...cargo?"

"It would be my honour," Sanek said loudly. More people had gathered, and standing above them on the seat of his cart, Sanek spread his arms wide. He looked like a performer, or a shopkeeper displaying his wares. "I disturbed the Beast by accident while mining in the Northern Mountains near my home village of Hartsbridge," he said. "It attacked, and I was forced to fight for my life. It was terrifying, and I was almost killed – but thankfully, I managed to chop off one of its legs using a pickaxe. Then I knocked it out with a club, before setting fire to its remains."

Tom frowned. He had so many questions, he hardly knew where to start. "Are you sure the Beast was Evil?" he asked. "There are many Good Beasts who might attack if surprised."

The man snorted. "When set upon by a vile monster, you don't ask its intentions! If I had stopped to chat with this creature, it would be rampaging through the villages of my home as we speak. No. I did what

I had to do…" He turned to the king and queen, and bowed again. "And now, I humbly ask Your Majesties for my reward."

Aroha turned to Hugo, eyebrows raised. "Do you know what reward he means?"

Hugo, his eyes on the blackened skeleton behind the man, nodded. "It is an ancient Avantian tradition that if a commoner slays an Evil Beast, he is richly rewarded." Hugo turned his attention to Sanek. "I will have a chest filled with gold and precious jewels to show the kingdom's appreciation for your bravery."

"Thank you, Your Majesty," Sanek said. "And if I could also trouble your boy there for some food and drink? It

has been a long journey."

"Of course!" Hugo said, turning
to Tom. Tom gaped back at the king
for a moment, before understanding

dawned on him. *Sanek thinks I'm a servant!* Tom opened his mouth to protest, but seeing Hugo's brows lower, he closed it again.

"I'll bring them at once, Your Majesty," Tom mumbled, then turned to go, his face burning with humiliation. As he headed towards the palace, Elenna stepped to his side.

"What did you make of Sanek's story?" she whispered. "Daltec and I don't think it adds up."

"It sounds pretty suspicious to me," Tom said. "I think I'll go to the stables and see if I can have a word with his son. He might know something useful."

"We're going to check in the library," said Elenna. "There must be some mention of a Beast near the village of Hartsbridge in one of the books."

But when Tom got to the stables, he found Sanek's horse already brushed and watered, tucking into a nosebag full of corn. The young boy was nowhere to be seen. Tom let out a growl of frustration. *There's more to Sanek's story than he's letting on, and I mean to find out the truth. But first...* Tom forced himself to stand tall and unclench his jaw. *I have serving duties to fulfil...*

3

UNANSWERED QUESTIONS

Elenna scanned a page of the huge book open on the table before her. At her side, Daltec riffled through another volume of the *Chronicles of Avantia*. So far they'd found nothing about a Beast near to Hartsbridge. More books were piled on the table, waiting to be consulted. Reaching the end of her volume, Elenna snapped it

closed, sending up a puff of dust.

"This is like looking for a needle in a haystack!" she said.

Daltec ran his finger along a shelf of books and sighed. "And one of the volumes is missing!" he said. "Maybe we should take a break – I'll have a stern word with the librarian later!"

"Agreed!" Elenna said, standing. "Let's see how Tom's getting on."

When Elenna and Daltec reached the palace courtyard they found Sanek seated at one of the banqueting tables laid ready for the next day. A feast of chicken and fruit was set before him, along with a half-finished jug of wine.

Nearby, Captain Harkman stood watching, lip curled in distaste as his men were unloading the bones of the Beast and rebuilding its skeleton in the middle of the courtyard.

"Surely it would be better to bury it?" said Elenna.

"I can't argue there," Harkman said, "but Sanek wanted it displayed as a gift to Prince Thomas, and I don't think Hugo wanted to disappoint him – the man's a hero, after all."

Elenna looked doubtfully across at their unexpected guest, noisily guzzling a cup of wine. *A strange kind of hero*, she thought. Sanek's son stood silently in the shadows behind his father, while Tom waited at his elbow with a napkin draped over one arm. *Poor Tom!*

Sanek munched on a leg of chicken, smacking his greasy lips together. Elenna looked again at the small, sandy-haired boy behind the miner, staring at his father's dinner as if he hadn't seen food for days.

"We have plenty more food at the palace," Elenna told Sanek as she and Daltec approached his table. "Certainly enough for both you and your son."

"Eh?" the man said, looking up.

"Your boy?" Elenna said. "Surely he needs refreshments also?"

"Don't worry about him," the man said. "He's not a big eater." But he tossed the lad the bone he'd almost

chewed clean. Elenna watched as
the child caught the chicken leg
and, after a fearful glance at Sanek,
started to nibble at it. She shook her
head in disgust. *The boy's afraid of his
own father!* Sanek drained the rest of

his glass of wine and held the empty vessel before Tom. "More wine!"

Elenna saw Tom flush red, but he carefully refilled the glass.

"Lift the Beast's head up higher!" Sanek called to Harkman's men as they positioned the skull. "Open its jaws. You'll see its teeth better then."

"What do you think of Thomas's latest birthday gift?" Elenna asked Tom, frowning as she gestured to the Beast skeleton. It was certainly a fearsome sight.

Tom shrugged. "It doesn't seem right," he said. "That was a living creature – Good or Evil, it shouldn't be treated like a trophy to be gawked at."

"I agree," said Elenna. Nevertheless, a handful of palace servants had come to watch the skeleton's construction, as well as several courtiers who had arrived early for the party the next day. A slender young man with a feathered hat noticed Tom and Elenna looking his way.

"Tell me, Tom," he called. "Have you ever faced a Beast this big?"

"A few," Tom answered. "Some bigger. But the size of a Beast doesn't always reflect how dangerous it is."

Sanek turned sharply to Tom, brows raised in astonishment.

"*You've* fought Beasts?" he said incredulously.

Tom sighed. "I'm actually the kingdom's Master of the Beasts."

Sanek snorted with laughter. "No!" he said, standing up to tower over

Tom. "I would have expected someone older for such an important role!"

Elenna's temper flared. "I assure you, Tom has defeated more Beasts than I care to count," she said. "And what's more, he doesn't feel the need to display them for all to see – or to demand a reward, either!"

"How *commendable*," Sanek said, seating himself again at the table. He looked at Tom, then smirked and shook his head as if he couldn't believe his eyes. "Master of the Beasts? Well, I never…"

It was almost more than Elenna could bear. She bit her tongue to stop herself saying something she'd regret.

"Hey! I have a splendid idea," the young man with the feathered hat cried. "How about a joust between our Beast conquerors, in honour of the prince's birthday? One doesn't often get the chance to see two such brave warriors fight. How about it? Tom versus Sanek!"

Tom shuffled his feet, his brow furrowed. Elenna knew he hated being hailed as a hero even more than being treated like a servant.

"It wouldn't be fair," she said. "Tom's been in lots of competitions. Sanek would be at a disadvantage."

Sanek shrugged. "I'm not afraid, if that's what you think. What I lack in technique, I suspect I'll more than make up for in strength. I'd be very willing to take on the challenge!"

Seeing Tom's frown deepen, Elenna

tried to help her friend again. "*I've* never jousted before," she said. "How about you face me? Then it would be a fair fight."

"Me? Joust a…a *girl*?" Sanek said, his eyes popping wide with outrage.

Elenna held her temper for Tom's sake. "I've battled pirates and Beasts," she said. "I'll put up a good fight."

"I'm sorry, but where I come from, we don't expect our women to defend our honour!" Sanek said.

"Joust! Joust! Joust!" cried the people around the Beast's skeleton.

Tom shrugged. "Fine! I accept your challenge," he said. But, looking at her friend's flushed cheeks and tense shoulders, Elenna thought she had rarely seen him more uncomfortable.

A HERO FALLS

Tom's spirits sank as he led Storm
towards the jousting lists. In the
time it had taken him to put on his
Golden Armour, a huge crowd had
gathered in the tournament field.
King Hugo sat on the new royal dais,
while the seating behind was packed
with nobles and palace staff. Storm
whickered softly. Holding his horse's
bridle, Tom sensed the stallion's

nervous tension. He patted Storm's neck, noticing the new grey hairs that flecked his horse's black coat.

"It's been a while, hasn't it, boy?" Tom said, trying to remember the last time they had jousted together. "I know you'll make me proud."

Cheers went up as Sanek rode into place at the far end of the jousting list. He had borrowed a piebald mare called Lady that Tom knew had a gentle temperament. But she looked skittish, the whites of her eyes showing. As Sanek tried to line her up by the fencing, she flinched back, tossing her head. Tom frowned as the big man kicked Lady hard in the ribs, yanking her head up with the reins.

Seeing Captain Harkman striding

towards him with his lance, Tom leapt up on to Storm's back. Elenna reached Tom at the same time as the captain.

"Good luck!" she said, patting Storm's side as Harkman handed Tom the lance. "Not that you'll need it!"

"Show him what a real Master of the Beasts can do!" Harkman added.

Tom tucked the lance under his right arm. At the far end of the barrier, Sanek was fumbling with his own weapon, letting the tip swing wildly as he tried to settle it under his arm.

"Well, being a miner by trade, I've never done this before!" the man said loudly, finally tucking the lance in place. "But it can't be harder than slaying a Beast. I'll give it my best shot!" Beyond Sanek, Tom could see about half the royal guard gathered in a group, exchanging what looked like notes and coins. *They're placing bets!* Tom straightened his spine and adjusted his lance. *Well, I don't intend to let them down!*

Tom sat poised, ready to charge. As he focussed on Sanek's broad chest, a hush fell over the field. Beside King Hugo, a bugle bearer brought his horn to his lips, sounding a short note.

Tom put his heels to his stallion's sides. Soon the rhythm of Storm's galloping hooves pulsed through Tom's body. At the far end of the track, Sanek kicked Lady into action.

The crowd roared as the two horses drew close...

Tom lowered his lance, bracing himself for his opponent's strike. *Whoa!* Storm suddenly stumbled and lurched to one side, sending Tom flying from the saddle. He landed heavily in a crunch of armour, his lance shattering beneath him.

Tom rolled over, and heaved himself up. His cheeks burned with shame, but he was more worried for Storm. Relief washed over him as he saw the stallion already standing – but his gait looked uneven. *He's thrown a shoe!* On the other side of the fence, Sanek drew up and flipped up his visor. Tom's opponent grinned down at him.

"Perhaps your horse was dazzled by your armour," Sanek sniggered, then trotted off again. Tom took hold of Storm's reins and lifted his foot for a closer look. Every nail that had fastened the shoe had rusted through.

"Impossible," he muttered. The shoes were only a few days old!

Storm let out a sad whinny as one

of Harkman's men arrived, leading
a new horse – a chestnut mare. "It's
not your fault," Tom said, rubbing a
comforting hand over his stallion's
mane. The man led Storm away, and

Tom leapt up on to his new steed.

"Come on, Tom! Do us proud!" Harkman said, handing Tom a fresh lance. Back at the far end of the list, Sanek punched his lance skywards, to a chorus of cheers.

Tom moved into position and gazed around at the guards and nobles, the king on his throne... *This time, I'll really show them what I can do!*

The bugle sounded again, and Tom set off, shouts and the thunder of hoofbeats loud in his ears. Not far along, the lance under his arm began to dip, strangely off-balance. It felt suddenly too heavy at the tip. *What's going on?* Tom adjusted his grip, bracing his muscles against the odd weight, but the weapon dipped further, as if something were pulling it down. Lady raced towards him, drawing close. Sanek's own weapon pointed straight and true. Tom struggled in the saddle, trying to keep his seat while fighting to lift his lance. It was hopeless. With a final, desperate heave, he tried to right it…

CRASH! Sanek's lance slammed into Tom's chest, flinging him from the saddle. He thudded down on his back, his head smashing against the inside of his helmet. For a few moments, he struggled to get his breath. Stunned and confused, with his ears ringing, Tom pushed himself up to a sitting position. He blinked to see Sanek standing over him, holding out a hand. Tom let his opponent pull

him up as the cheers of the crowd rushed back to him in a dizzying wave, then hauled off his helmet.

"You took quite a knock there," Sanek said, eyes twinkling. "D'you need to lie down?"

"The lance," said Tom, struggling to regain his composure. "Something was wrong. It was too heavy."

Sanek sneered. "Maybe use a child's one next time, eh?"

Tom bit back his rage and stood up, before offering a short bow to Sanek. He just wanted to get away as quickly as possible. "Congratulations on your victory," he managed. Then he turned and stalked off. He saw disappointment in the soldiers' gazes as they handed money to a few nobles who had clearly bet against him.

I let everyone down, Tom thought. His shoulders slumped, his Golden Armour suddenly weighing heavily on him. *And I let myself down. But how?*

The enormous Beast skeleton dominated the now largely empty courtyard. Tom was about to pass by when something caught his eye, and he paused. The creature was huge, with curved pointed feet like giant talons, but it was the legs that drew his attention. He looked closely.

Sanek said he cut one off with an axe. But none of the bones show any marks. Maybe I'm misremembering. Or maybe Sanek isn't being entirely honest...

Glancing back towards the noisy

tournament field, Tom considered returning to challenge the man. *No...* He let out a sigh. *I can't do that. I'll just look like a sore loser. I need proof. But, while there's blood in my veins, I will find out what Sanek's up to!*

1

MESSAGE IN A BOTTLE

Tom stood in his chamber with
Elenna and Daltec, gazing out at the
dusky courtyard. All the tables and
benches had now been set up, ready
for the feasting next day, but the huge
Beast skeleton at the centre stood
over everything. Torches had been
lit all around it, and in the flickering
light, the vast skeleton almost seemed

to move. Taking in the creature's long fangs and jointed limbs, each tipped with a single, dagger-like claw, Tom knew it would have been a horrifying opponent. It just didn't seem likely that anyone – even a big man like Sanek – would have been able to defeat it with just a pickaxe. *And he shouldn't have been able to beat me in the joust, either!*

Elenna put her hand on his shoulder. "Are you all right?" she asked.

"Not really," Tom said. "I don't trust Sanek at all. I'm pretty sure he used some sort of magic against me in the joust – Storm's shoe rusted through in moments, and my lance had a mind of its own. If he has access to magical powers, that might explain how he killed a Beast single-handed… But I can't warn King Hugo without looking like I'm sulking."

"We should keep a close eye on our guest from now on," Elenna said.

A knock on the door made them all turn.

"Come in," said Daltec, but no one entered. Frowning, Tom crossed the room and opened the door, but the torchlit passage was empty. *Strange!* A water flask lay just outside. Tom picked it up and turned to show the others.

"Someone left this," he said. "It feels too light to have water inside."

"Open it, but be cautious," Daltec said. "It could contain something poisonous." Tom held the flask well

away from his face and held his
breath as he gently eased the stopper
out. Nothing happened. He tipped
it upside down, and a small roll of
parchment fell out on to the floor. He

picked it up, unrolling it as he walked back to the others. It was a note, roughly printed in what looked like charcoal. Elenna and Daltec leaned in to read:

Sanek isn't who he seems to be. Go to Hartsbridge to find out the truth.

"Looks like our instincts were correct," said Tom.

"Who could have left it?" Elenna asked.

"I don't recognise the writing," Daltec said, peering closely. "But there are so many visitors in the palace at the moment, it could be from just about anyone."

"Someone who knows more about

Sanek than we do," Tom said. "But one thing's for sure, he can't be trusted. I think we should do what the note suggests. Daltec, can you transport me to Hartsbridge?"

"It might be a trick to get rid of you," Elenna warned.

"Elenna's right," Daltec said, "but I think we need to investigate anyway. If Sanek is able to use magic, he could be dangerous. And right now, he's worked his way into the heart of the palace. Tom, I think you and I should go together. That way, I can magic us straight back here if something goes wrong."

"Good plan," Elenna said. "I'll stay here and keep an eye on Sanek."

"Don't tell the king we've gone,

though," Tom said. "I don't want him thinking I'm a bad sport."

"I don't believe His Majesty would think that for a second, Tom," Elenna said. "But I'll cover for you. Just get back here by morning, because if you don't turn up for Thomas's birthday party, everyone will wonder why."

"We'll be back by dawn," Tom said. "I promise."

"So, Hartsbridge it is, then," Daltec said, clapping his hands. "Are you ready?"

With his sword in its sheath, and his shield on his back, Tom nodded.

"Then close your eyes," Daltec said. "Or you're likely to get dizzy."

Tom did as he was told, and Daltec began chanting under his breath. Tom felt a cool breeze stir his hair, a tug at his stomach, and the ground shifted under his feet...

"We're here!" Daltec said. Tom opened his eyes to find a dark, rugged landscape of high mountains spread before him under a starry sky. A small village, little more than a handful of houses, was nestled just ahead in the crook between the two closest mountains – but every window was dark, and no smoke issued from the chimneys.

"Either people here go to bed very early," Daltec said, "or the place is abandoned. Maybe Sanek was telling the truth, and everyone fled because of the Beast?"

"Let's take a closer look, to make

sure," Tom said, setting off along the narrow track leading between the dark, timber buildings of the village. Though every door was shut, the silence was broken by the occasional bark of a dog. As Tom passed a wooden coop, he heard the soft cluck of roosting chickens inside. *The people here left in a hurry.*

"Look!" Daltec whispered, as they rounded a bend. Where he pointed, a single light shone from a ground-floor window of one of the houses. Tom approached the door and knocked. It opened a crack, letting out a sliver of light, and a fair-haired, middle-aged man with pallid skin and sunken eyes peered out. Behind him, Tom could just make out a woman, her dark hair tied up in a bun.

"What do you want?" the man asked, eyes narrowed suspiciously.

"We've come from the City," Tom said. "We're not here to cause trouble.

We just want to talk. And we'd
be happy to reward you for any
information you have…about Sanek."

The man looked wary, but opened
the door wider. "You'd better come
in," he said.

"Take a seat by the fire, I'll make
you some tea," the woman said,
smiling now as she brushed down her
crumpled brown dress. "And don't
mind Ivan – we just don't get many
visitors…"

"Thank you," Tom said. A pair of
chairs sat beside the fire. Tom took
one and Daltec the other, while Ivan
went to help his wife at the stove.

"So, word must have spread about
Sanek's bravery," the woman said,
as she measured tea into a pot. She

seemed nervous, her hand shaking. "About how he stabbed a Beast through the heart to protect the village and saved us all."

"Through the heart?" Tom asked. "I heard that he cut the head off the Beast."

The woman shot him a quick glance. "Well, yes, that's right," she said hurriedly. "First, he stabbed it through the heart, *then* he cut off its head." Something in her look, and the quick way she had answered, made Tom doubt she was telling the truth. But the woman smiled brightly as she brought two steaming cups over and handed one to Tom and one to Daltec. Ivan seated himself at a table nearby with his own cup.

"Sanek's a hero," he said. "Everyone would have perished if it weren't for him."

Tom's cup was chipped, and the tea inside looked murky – but not wanting to insult his hosts, he took a sip. It tasted very sweet. Across from him, Daltec sipped from his own mug.

"Now, is there anything else we can help you with?" the woman asked.

"Yes," said Tom. But when he opened his mouth to speak again, no words came. *What was I going to say?* His head suddenly felt like it had been filled with water, his vision blurring. He blinked his eyes. With a clatter, Daltec dropped his mug to the floor, then slumped forward in his chair. *He's passed out!*

"What have you given us?" said Tom, setting his own cup down.

"I'm sorry," the woman said sadly. Tom fumbled for his sword and tried to rise, but his fingers had no strength to grip the hilt. The room swam around him. Black spots crawled at the edge of his vision and he toppled forwards, darkness enveloping him before he hit the ground.

SNOOPING

Early next morning, the smell of
bread baking and meat roasting
filled the courtyard as Elenna dodged
between palace staff busy making
last-minute preparations for the feast.
She had already tried Tom's room and
found it empty – Daltec's, too. She
chewed her lip. *What could have kept
them from returning? Something to
do with Sanek?* A young kitchen girl

Elenna knew well passed in front of her, carrying two pails of milk.

"Sara!" Elenna called. The girl stopped and bobbed a quick curtsy, almost sloshing her milk on the floor.

"How can I help, miss?" the girl asked.

"I was hoping you might be able to tell me something about Sanek and his son. Does anything strike you as strange about them?"

Sara tipped her head, thinking. "Sanek enjoys the finer things in life – wine and cheese and the like. He's even got the king's own tailor to make him a new outfit for the feast. His boy doesn't talk much, though. And we're not allowed to go into their rooms, even to set the fire. But maybe, because

they're common folk, they're used to
looking after themselves."

"Hmm… Maybe. Thank you, Sara,
that's very helpful," Elenna said,
although the girl's words had made

her more uneasy than ever. *Sanek likes people waiting on him, but he doesn't want them in his room – that sounds suspicious...*

"Elenna?" Captain Harkman called as he strode towards her. "Have you seen Tom? He's supposed to be helping me drill the soldiers for a display later, but he hasn't turned up!"

"Ah..." Elenna thought quickly. "Actually, I was just coming to tell you. He's very badly bruised from the joust yesterday, so he was hoping you could get by without him."

Captain Harkman's forehead creased in pity. "He did get rather a beating, didn't he? Poor lad. Let him know I can manage."

"If young Tom can't handle the heat, I'm happy to volunteer as Master of the Beasts," a brash voice said from behind Elenna. She turned to see Sanek and his son. The tall man had changed from his brown and beige work clothes into a red outfit with gilt brocade and gleaming buttons. "After all, Avantia needs someone who looks the part," he said, giving his cloak a swish. "Not to mention, someone who can handle a lance." Harkman frowned, and looked about to jump to Tom's defence. Elenna beat him to it, having a sudden idea.

"Tom can manage just fine, thank you!" she said. "He doesn't need flashy clothes to prove his worth. He's descended from Taladon the Swift.

In fact, if you want to find out more about his lineage, you should visit the Gallery of Tombs."

"What a splendid idea!" Harkman said. "I can show you the way now, if you like?"

"I'm not sure how interesting a few old graves will be," Sanek said.

"I want to see Taladon's tomb!" the boy piped up, his eyes shining at the idea. "Mother used to tell me stories about Taladon and—"

"Fine," Sanek said, cutting the boy off. "We'll take a look. But mind you keep quiet – we're visiting the dead, after all."

Once Harkman had led Sanek and his boy towards the entrance to the catacombs, Elenna hurried back inside the palace. *I won't have long!* She strode purposefully through the palace corridors, trying her best to look natural, and had soon reached Sanek's chamber. Normally she would never consider what she was about to do, but she was certain Sanek's story was bogus. Elenna took a deep breath, looked both ways and tried the handle. *Locked...of course.* She took a spare arrowhead from her pocket, slipping the tip into the lock mechanism. It took a fair bit of jiggling, but finally, she heard the latch click. *Yes!*

Stomach bubbling with nerves, Elenna slipped inside, shutting the door softly behind her.

The room was almost bare, with

just a water jug on the washstand
and a plate of fruit on a table.
Elenna crossed to the bed and peered
underneath, but found nothing except
the chamber pot. Sanek's old brown
clothes and a riding cloak hung inside
the wardrobe, but there was no sign
of a weapon or staff. Elenna checked
on top of the wardrobe, behind the
dresser, even under the bedclothes.
Still nothing. Disappointed, she
was about to leave, when an acrid
tang caught in her throat. Smoke
– but not normal woodsmoke. She
glanced towards the fireplace to see
something odd smouldering among
the embers – the charred remains of a
leather-bound book.

Bending for a closer look, Elenna

made out gilt writing on the front. *Oh my!* It was the missing volume of the *Chronicles of Avantia*. But what was it doing here? She gingerly picked the smoking book up between two fingers and hurried to the nightstand. There she carefully poured some water from the jug on to the smouldering part.

As Elenna tucked the book under her arm to leave, she heard footsteps approaching from outside. Her heart leapt, and she looked for somewhere to hide. *Under the bed? No! What if they want to use the pot?*

A key rattled in the lock. Elenna made a dash for the window and clambered on to the sill.

"That's odd..." Elenna heard Sanek say. "I must have forgotten to lock it."

She climbed out of the window and shuffled along the ledge outside. The turrets and sloping rooftops of the palace spread before her, and far below, people moved around, looking as tiny as insects. Elenna swallowed hard.

She heard the door creak open and two sets of footsteps enter the room as she pressed her body against the stonework. The bow and arrows stowed on her back and the book clutched to her front made balancing tricky. A strong breeze had picked up, and each time a gust blasted against her, all her muscles tensed. *Hold tight… Don't fall…*

"Can you smell wet ashes?" Sanek asked, then let out a growl. "I told the maid not to come in here! If someone's been meddling, I'll make them pay!"

"I can't smell anything," a young

boy's voice answered. "And I don't understand why we can't go back home, now that you've got your reward."

"This isn't about treasure, Jamil," Sanek snapped. "It's about revenge. I'm just starting to enjoy myself. Unless you've got anything useful to add, keep your mouth shut! I don't want to hear you utter a single word outside this chamber again, do you hear me?"

"Yes," Jamil answered. Another gust of wind tugged at Elenna's clothes and hair. She wanted to stay longer, but if they looked out of the window now, they might see her. Instead, she tucked the book into the front of her tunic and looked upwards towards

Aduro's tower. *I wish I had Tom's golden boots*, she thought.

Elenna took a deep breath, then started to climb the almost smooth

brickwork, wedging her fingers and toes into chinks in the mortar. Sharp gusts threatened to pull her to her death, and her heart hammered painfully against her ribs. By the time she reached Aduro's shuttered window, her arms trembled from the effort. Balancing both feet on a narrow piece of decorative brickwork, she reached up and knocked on the shutter. *Please be in!*

A moment later, the shutters flew open and Aduro's head poked out, his long white beard almost tickling her face.

"Down here!" Elenna hissed. When he looked down, Aduro's sharp eyes shot wide open at the sight of Elenna clinging to the brickwork. "I need your help," she whispered.

"Well, I suppose you'd better come in, then," Aduro said.

RUNNING OUT OF TIME

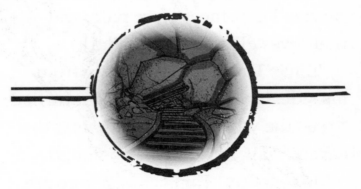

Tom opened his eyes a crack to find himself in near darkness. A deep, bone-aching cold had soaked into his body while he slept, and now every muscle felt stiff. Bound together at the wrists, his hands felt almost numb. *Elenna was right – we've walked straight into a trap!*

As his eyes adjusted to the light of a

few candles, he made out the figures of people sitting all around him, huddled together in an underground cavern. Their faces were pale, and their eyes glittered in the dark.

"Tom?" Daltec said croakily from his side. "Are you awake?" Tom turned to see the wizard leaning against the cavern wall, his hands also bound.

"Just about," Tom said. "Where are we?"

"Some sort of mine, I would guess," Daltec said, nodding towards a cart in the middle of the cave, on a set of iron tracks. Tom gazed at the people all around him – grubby, gaunt, wide-eyed with fear. Then he spotted a pair of familiar faces – the couple who had drugged him. He gritted his teeth,

but as soon as the woman saw him
looking her way, she dipped her head.

"We're so sorry," the woman said
hurriedly. "We had no choice."

"Truly," her husband added, and

Tom noticed the man was shaking – with fear or cold, he couldn't tell. "If there was any way we could make it up to you, we would."

Tom's anger faded at once. *They're trapped too. There must be someone else behind all this. But who?*

"You can start by telling us what's going on," Daltec said, gently.

The woman looked down. "A woman came to our village," she said. "We thought she was a collector looking for precious stones. She promised to pay us each enough gold to last a lifetime, if we would just dig into the mountain for her, following a map she had drawn. She wouldn't tell us what she was looking for – she just said we would know when we found it."

"And we did know," the man cut in. "It was the remains of a Beast, with teeth as long as my arm. 'Arkano', she called it. She had us load the skeleton into a cart. After that, she put on a feast for the whole village with roast pork and wine. But the wine was drugged. We all woke up in here."

"She collapsed the entrance so no one can escape," the woman said. "But she has a way of transporting herself and other people in and out. We think she might be a sorceress of some sort."

That doesn't sound good.

The woman had begun to cry. "We had to do what she said, because she has our son, Jamil." She dashed the tears away. "I can't bear to think what she might do to our boy. And now we'll never see him again."

"I'll do everything in my power to get him back to you," Tom said. But it didn't all yet make sense.

"What would a sorceress want with a dead Beast?" asked Daltec. "And how does Sanek fit into all this? Did he steal the Beast from her to pretend he killed it and get the reward?"

"We've never actually met him," the woman said. "The witch told us, if anyone asked, Sanek is a hero who slayed the Beast and saved us."

Tom and Daltec exchanged a look. "Sounds like Sanek is nothing but this sorceress's puppet!" Tom said.

A blinding white light flooded the cave. "That's where you're wrong!" a familiar voice said gleefully. "He's far

more than that." When Tom's eyes had
recovered, he saw a familiar young
woman before him, her red hair in
a mohawk style, a pierced eyebrow
arched as she grinned at him.

"Ria," Tom sighed. "Why am I not
surprised that you're behind this?"

Ria strode over to stand above Tom, looking down with a sneer. "I just *knew* you'd have to come sniffing around," she said.

"What are you playing at?" Tom snarled. "And who is Sanek?"

"Wouldn't you like to know?" Ria said. "The poor souls in the City will find out soon enough, though, when a Beast attacks them with no brave little Tommikins to save the day! You, on the other hand, will die slowly and horribly, just as soon as these candles burn up all the air in the cavern." She clicked her fingers, and at least twenty more candles lit up all around the cave. "I almost wish I could stick around to watch, but... Well, I've got a Beast to wake up!" With another click of her fingers, Ria vanished.

What Beast? Tom thought. *Arkano is dead!* But with the air fast running out, he didn't have time to wonder.

He hurried towards the nearest candle and held his bound wrists over the flame. The pain of his flesh singeing made him catch his breath, but he ignored it, quickly burning through the rope. *I can heal the burns later. Right now, I have a job to do!* Free of his bonds, Tom tried to blow the candle out, but it sputtered, and burned brighter. *Evil Magic!*

Tom quickly untied Daltec, then turned to the villagers, who had been watching mutely. "Show us the blocked entrance," he said.

"This way," said the woman who

had drugged him. She led Tom and Daltec to where the tracks vanished, buried under a huge mound of rubble. Tom's heart sank. Even with the strength of his golden breastplate, he wouldn't be able to shift the rocks, and his sword could never hack through so much stone. He yawned suddenly, then shook his head to clear the fuzziness. Fear jolted through him. *I'm already feeling the lack of air!* Looking around, he saw villagers starting to sag, their eyelids drooping. Daltec blinked and shook his head as if he too was struggling to stay awake.

Tom racked his brains for an escape plan. But all he could think of was how they would all suffocate, trapped underground while everyone in the

City would be at the mercy of Ria
and whatever Beast she'd found.
One of the enchanted candles died,
dimming the cave. Then another. Tom
swallowed hard.

*It won't be long before our lives are
extinguished too...*

1

STORY TWO

I've done the only thing I could think to make a difference – a tiny chance to save us all. If Sanek finds out what I've done, I'm dead. But if no one gets my message, we're all dead anyway. If only I could just go home and see my mother and father one last time. If I get out of this alive, I'll never complain about having to help with mucking out the animals again. I'm putting all my faith and hope in the Master of the Beasts. In Mother's tales, they always knew what to do – they always defeated the Beast in the end. But this isn't a story. I can only hope Tom is braver and more powerful than Sanek says he is.

Jamil

CONFRONTING SANEK

Elenna leaned over Aduro's shoulder as he carefully prised apart the damp pages of the scorched book on his desk.

The old man sighed and pointed to the stubby edges of torn sheets near the spine. "Who would treat a book like this? A whole section has been ripped out!"

"Someone who's trying to hide something," Elenna said.

Aduro craned forward suddenly. "Ah! Now, this is interesting!" he said, running a finger down the next intact page. "The missing section refers to a

time where Marlon was Master of the Beasts. This might be helpful."

"How?" said Elenna, looking at the smudged ink. "I can't read it at all!"

Aduro stroked his beard. "As well as being a warrior, Marlon was a keen scholar, and wrote his *own* account of his Quests. So, if we can find Marlon's works, we might understand why this section has been removed."

"If Sanek doesn't find them first," Elenna said. "Of course, Tom may already have the information we need…" At Aduro's puzzled look, Elenna explained about the message in the flask, and Tom and Daltec's mission. Aduro's ancient, lined face creased further.

"King Hugo has been mightily

deceived," he said, shaking his head. "He thinks Sanek's a hero, when in fact, he's a trickster. But until we have proof of his intentions, we can do nothing."

Elenna jabbed a finger at the book on the table. "Surely that's proof enough?" she said. "I'm taking it to Hugo now, before Sanek can do any more harm!"

"I think it would be better to wait until Tom returns, or until we have uncovered Marlon's works," Aduro said. "After all, we don't want Sanek to realise we're on to him, not before we have proof he stole the book."

"Tom promised he'd be back at dawn," Elenna protested. "Something's already happened to him. We can't wait. I'm going to see Hugo now and I'm taking Sanek with me – at arrow-point if I have to!"

Elenna stormed from the room. Aduro shuffled after her, but she didn't wait for him. She checked Sanek's chamber to find he had already left. Back in the courtyard, preparations for the feast were almost complete. Trestle tables had been laid; kitchen staff wearing immaculate white aprons were putting out baskets of bread and fruit; a band was setting up nearby. Elenna spotted Sanek standing at the centre of a crowd of nobles near the Beast skeleton. He was swinging a shiny new sword set with jewels.

"I'll have the smith engrave the

Beast's likeness on the scabbard,"
Sanek was saying as Elenna
approached.

"Move!" Elenna told the gathered
nobles, unhooking her bow and
nocking an arrow. The crowd parted,

and Sanek held up his hands defensively.

"What are you doing, child?" he asked. "Put that thing away, before you wound someone!"

"Not until I've heard the truth!" Elenna snapped. "What was one of the *Chronicles of Avantia* doing half burned in your fireplace?"

Sanek's eyes widened in bewilderment. "I don't know what you mean. I'm a man of action – I have no interest in *stories*. And why would anyone burn a book?"

"You tell us," said Aduro, arriving at her back and holding the charred volume aloft for all to see. "We have the proof here!"

Sanek blinked in surprise, then

frowned down at Jamil. "Tell me the truth now, son. Since I know nothing of this matter, it must be down to you."

"I...I..." Jamil looked up at the big man, then at Elenna, his shoulders hunched up round his ears and his small frame shaking with fear. "I borrowed it to read about the heroes!" he blurted.

"Thief!" Sanek roared, drawing back a hand to strike the child. Elenna caught the big man's wrist as Jamil cringed away from the blow.

"Are you telling the truth?" she asked the boy. "You stole this book?"

Jamil looked anxiously up at Sanek, then nodded.

"But why burn it?" Elenna asked.

"That makes no sense."

"While I was reading, I spilled some food on it," Jamil said. "I thought I'd get into trouble, so I tried to get rid of it so no one would know."

Elenna didn't believe a word. "And you tore a bunch of pages out too, I suppose?"

"I know what this is really about!" Sanek shouted. "I beat that weakling runt, and he's put you up to this. What's his name? Tim? You've both been against me since the moment I arrived – jealous that someone else has served their kingdom by defeating a Beast!"

"Don't be ridiculous!" Elenna snapped. "Why would we be jealous of a lying cheat? We know you tampered with Storm's shoe in the joust, and that you did something to *Tom's* lance – stop playing the innocent."

Sanek gaped at her. "This is madness!" he cried. "I'm a simple miner, not some kind of warlock!"

"What's the matter?" Captain Harkman said gruffly as he approached.

"This!" Elenna said, gesturing to the remains of the old volume. "Sanek stole it and tried to burn it. I found it in the fire in his room!"

"Is this true?" Harkman asked, turning to the man.

"As we have already explained," Sanek said, "Jamil borrowed the book and tried to burn it after accidentally damaging it. And *I'd* like to know, is

it standard practice here to send spies
sneaking into an honoured guest's
private chambers?"

"Well, no—" Harkman started, but
Elenna cut him off.

"He's obviously been hiding something since he arrived, and this is the proof," Elenna snapped. "He's a liar and a thief, and who knows what else!"

Sanek puffed up his chest, his eyes flashing with fury. "I have never been so insulted in my life. Captain – are you going to let this *child* speak to me this way?"

Elenna gritted her teeth and glared as Harkman looked between her and Sanek, his brow furrowed.

"Look," he said, "everyone is clearly upset and confused, but this isn't the time for arguments. Prince Thomas's birthday celebration is about to begin, so I ask that you both stay calm. I'm sure we'll soon get to the bottom of the matter."

"I'm not in the least bit confused!"
Elenna said. "For Thomas's sake,
I'll let this rest for now. But I *won't*
forget about it!" She stalked away,
past Aduro.

"Speaking of Thomas, where *is* our
young Master of the Beasts?" Sanek
called after her. "Too ashamed to
show his face?"

Elenna gritted her teeth and kept
walking. *I wish Tom were here!* she
thought. *If only there was some way
I could help him! Something terrible
must have happened to keep him and
Daltec from returning.*

A DESPERATE PLAN

In the cavern, an elderly villager collapsed forwards, his knees buckling. Tom and Daltec rushed to help, but a woman got there first, propping him up, patting his cheek to wake him. Another candle flickered out. Panic clawed at Tom, his chest tightening as if trapped in a Beast's deadly embrace. The villagers were all looking at him, their faces full of terror mixed with hope. *There must be a way to save us all! This place can't be our tomb.*

"Can you magic us out?" Tom asked the wizard. Daltec shook his head.

"I fear the walls are too thick for my spells. If my magic fails, you

might end up encased in stone!"

Tom glanced again at the huddled villagers. "Who knows this mine well?" he asked. "Surely there's another way out?"

A burly man with a thick, greying

beard and a barrel chest stepped forward. "I've mined these mountains for most of my life," he said. "This cave was abandoned long ago because it was too unstable. There was one way in, and one way out." He pointed towards the pile of rubble at the end of the tracks. "Now there's none."

Tom ran his eyes over the cave walls in desperation. He spotted large, blackened areas on the rock – scorch marks! *Parts of the cave must have been opened up with...*

"Explosives!" Tom said. "That's what we need!"

The bearded man looked at Tom as if he'd grown a second head. "I suppose that would be a quicker death," he said. "If we use explosives, the whole roof will come down. We'll be buried alive."

"But you do have some?" Tom asked.

The man nodded. "In that cart over there." Tom weighed up the options. With each flicker of the enchanted candles he grew weaker, his mind foggy. He could feel the sands of time running out. *If I don't at least try, we'll all die, and soon.* But it was a big risk.

Tom turned to Daltec and kept his voice low so as not to get the villagers' hopes up. "Can you create a forcefield strong enough to protect everyone here from falling rocks while I blow the entrance open?" he asked.

Daltec rubbed at his forehead. "There are too many of us in here for my spell to protect us all," he said at last. "But if

I enchant your shield, and you use the strength of heart of your breastplate too…that might just be enough."

It would have to be.

Tom nodded. "Be ready with your spell," he said. Then he turned back to the villagers. There were at least two dozen of them, some older than Aduro, the youngest an infant in his mother's arms. Tom cleared his throat.

"When I say, I want you all to gather around me as close as you can," he said, glad that his voice sounded steady. "I'll get us out of here alive!"

Tom crossed to the old wooden cart on its tracks leading towards the rubble-filled entrance. In the cart were four tubes of explosive powder, each with a fuse. *I hope they still work…*

Tom picked up the nearest candle, willing himself steady, then brought it towards the explosives. He hesitated. *Once I light it, there's no way back ...*

Then he took a shuddering breath and set his candle to the first fuse.

Nothing. It didn't even fizz. *Perhaps it's too old...*

In the silence, Tom could hear Daltec chanting softly, preparing his spell. He tried the second explosive.

Swoosh! This one spluttered into life. Tom quickly lit the third and the fourth, panic rising inside him...then he pushed the cart as hard as he could towards the mound of rocks.

"Now!" he cried, taking his shield from his back and lifting it over his head. Daltec put his hand to the shield.

Whumpf! The wood started to blaze like a furnace, shedding golden light around them. Some of the gathered people gasped and flinched back.

"To me!" Tom commanded. The villagers crowded close until everyone was inside the halo of light.

BOOM! The whole cavern leapt. Smoke and dust filled the air. Villagers screamed, clamping their hands over their ears. As the worst of the smoke cleared, Tom saw a new chink of light – a pale dawn ray, streaming into the cavern. The explosives had blown a hole, and it looked big enough to squeeze through!

"Head towards the light!" Tom cried, pointing. But as he said the words, a hideous grating groan filled

the chamber. *THUD!* Tom's knees almost buckled as a massive hunk of rock crashed down on to the forcefield surrounding his shield.

Tom forced himself to start moving towards the light, the villagers crowded tightly around him. With each step, more stone smashed down from above, each blow straining Tom's arms and back, his thighs and knees, until he could barely put one foot in front of the other. Stinging sweat ran into his eyes, and he could feel his bones being bent beneath the weight of the stone.

But the light grew steadily brighter, and the first of the villagers – the woman with her small child – squeezed out through the opening. More quickly followed. Tom could hardly stay upright. The agony in his limbs took over. The loud thud of the blood in his ears mixed with the crashes and booms all around, filling his senses. He couldn't see...

A hand gripped his arm.

"Tom!" Daltec cried. Tom shook himself. "All the villagers are out!" His friend was beckoning for him to follow. Tom lowered his shield so he would fit through the gap, and stumbled into daylight, just as a tremendous crash erupted behind him. He sank to the ground. A woman bent at his side, soon joined by a young man with anxious blue eyes. Then the mother with her baby.

"Thank you!" they were all saying. Tom let them tug him to his feet.

"There's no sign of Ria," said the young wizard. "We must return to the City! Now!"

ARKANO AWAKENS

Elenna leaned on the windowsill as gold and jewels were loaded into an enormous chest beside the skeleton of the Beast in the courtyard below. Sanek smiled and nodded as the people gathered around him clapped and cheered. The banquet was due to start any moment, and Tom and Daltec still weren't back. Elenna felt cold inside. There'd been no word at all.

She turned, about to go down to join the festivities, when her door suddenly opened. Aduro bundled inside, breathless, a slim volume in one hand.

"Quick! Come now," he said, beckoning her to follow as he swept out again, robes flying. "I have Marlon's writings. We must tell the king and queen!"

"Tell them what?"

But Aduro had already turned to go. Elenna hurried towards the ballroom after him, dread twisting in her stomach. She'd never seen the old man move so fast, or look so worried.

They burst into the heaving ballroom together. Queen Aroha and King Hugo sat on a raised dais at the back, dressed in matching cream and gold outfits. On the dancefloor, nobles ambled about sipping drinks. Baby Thomas sat on a plump lady's lap near the edge of the room, chewing on a little wooden sword.

As Aduro and Elenna hurried towards the dais, Aroha and Hugo looked up together, their smiles vanishing as they took in Aduro's expression.

"Your Majesties!" Aduro said. "You must send your strongest guards to surround the Beast's skeleton at once!"

Hugo frowned. "But, why? It's just a pile of charred bones."

"No! Listen…" Aduro opened the book in his hands and began to read aloud. "*A local man told me of a*

Beast lurking within the mountains
– a creature that could sleep for
centuries, appearing dead as a fossil.
It can only be awoken when fire
touches its cold heart, so they buried
it under the mountain, never to be
seen again. They called it Arkano, the
Stone Crawler..."

Elenna gasped, ice-cold horror washing over her. Hugo and Aroha still looked puzzled.

"Don't you see?" Elenna asked. "That thing in the courtyard is not dead. Sanek must have found the bones and brought them here to claim a reward. But flames could awaken it. And there are torches blazing everywhere down there, we must—"

Shouts from the courtyard below

cut off her words. Elenna tore across
the room, shouldering her way
between nobles until she reached the
window. Aduro quickly joined her,
along with the king and queen.

Below, at the centre of the
courtyard, a slender, hooded figure
stood in front of the skeleton, a knife
in one hand and a torch in the other.
Most of the guests and servants had
drawn back in terror, but Sanek stood
right beside the hooded form. A pair
of guards rushed towards the pair.
The slender figure with the torch
threw back her hood, and Elenna felt
suddenly sick.

Ria!

The girl smiled and lifted her hand,
still holding the knife, to wave at

Elenna and the others at the window.

"Shall I do it now, Mother?" Ria asked, glancing up at Sanek.

"'Mother'?" Elenna gasped, her stomach clenching with dread.

Sanek's features blurred. He seemed to grow thinner, shorter, his hair lengthening.

"A glamour spell!" Aduro muttered. Soon, a woman was gazing back at Elenna with piercing, taunting green eyes.

Kensa!

"Stop them!" Hugo called down to his guards. The two armoured men had almost reached the pair, but Ria lifted her torch and blew on the flame. With a roar, the fire billowed outwards in a white-hot flare towards

the guards, forcing them to stagger
away, shielding their faces. Servants
and guests alike fled for the shadows
with cries of alarm, while Ria threw
back her head and laughed.

"Do it!" Kensa cried. Still laughing,

Ria touched her flaming torch to the
skeleton. Instantly, the whole thing
kindled as if doused in oil. Through

the flames engulfing its body, Elenna saw a hardened crust cracking and flaking away, revealing red flesh that glowed like lava underneath. The redness swelled and melded together, filling the empty ribcage and fleshing out the bones until a hideous creature with countless glowing yellow eyes and a long, lashing tail stood where the skeleton had been. Elenna's chest tightened with horror as the Beast lifted its head and roared.

TURNED TO STONE

Tom opened his eyes to find himself just outside the City, transported there by Daltec's magic. Smoke rose above the palace walls, and terrified screams came from within.

"It sounds like we're not a moment too soon!" Daltec said. Tom and the wizard raced through the city gates and into the courtyard. Tom skidded to a stop. A huge, glowing, lizard-like creature crouched where Sanek's Beast skeleton had been, jaws open showing long, sharp teeth, and eyes blazing with fury. *Arkano!* Palace staff and banqueting guests ran for cover, but two familiar figures stood beside the huge reptile, grinning from ear to ear. *Ria... and Kensa! I should have guessed they'd be in this together!* Tom drew his sword and lunged towards them, but Kensa's head snapped around before he could reach her. The evil witch lifted a hand and hurled a bolt of silver energy towards Tom.

FIZZZZ! The bolt slammed into Tom's chest, throwing him backwards. Glassware and crockery crashed to

the ground as Tom slid over a table
and landed in a roll on the flagstones.
He scrambled up to see Kensa send
Daltec flying with another bolt.
The wizard hit the ground and lay
groaning, blood welling from a gash

on his temple. Beyond Kensa, Arkano lunged towards a pair of soldiers, lashing his huge tail from side to side, his clustered yellow eyes rolling and smoke pouring from his nostrils. Before the Beast could reach them, the soldiers scattered.

Tom was headed after the Beast, dodging between tables, when he heard the crash of doors being flung open. The Beast turned towards the sound as on the far side of the courtyard, Captain Harkman burst from the palace and charged, sword raised. Close behind the captain, Elenna emerged, leaping on to a table and firing an arrow at the vast lizard. But as the arrow hit Arkano's flesh, it burned away to ash. Tom vaulted over the table before him and raced between benches to reach the Beast, just as Harkman drew back his sword.

Towering over Harkman, Arkano sent out a plume of smoke, bathing the captain. To Tom's horror, Harkman's flesh turned a dull, stony grey. He managed a few more steps, but then froze solid, his face a rictus of fear. *No!* Tom's heart clenched with fear. The Beast lumbered on towards the palace.

Every one of Elenna's arrows burned away as soon as they touched Arkano's flesh, not slowing him at all. Tom raced after Arkano as he smashed everything in his path, before eventually reaching the palace wall.

Ha! Cornered! Tom thought. But instead of turning to fight him, the

Beast clambered up the wall on curved, talon-like feet. He turned to hiss angrily back at Elenna, who was still firing arrows, before clambering up on to the palace battlements.

The soldiers manning the walls took one look at the glowing monster and dived out of the way. One, though, remained at his post, turning a trebuchet loaded with a boulder. He was about to launch it towards the Beast, but Arkano puffed out a cloud of petrifying smoke, turning him and his war machine to stone. Elenna had rushed into a tower staircase, heading for the battlements herself.

Tom was about to follow, when a sudden searing pain in his shoulder snatched his breath away. He tried to move, but his muscles wouldn't obey. He craned his head around to see Kensa smirking, a bolt of sizzling light streaming from one finger, pinning him through the shoulder. Ria stepped from her mother's side and slowly stalked towards him, grinning as she strode through broken glass and crockery, a long, curved knife in her hand. Tom struggled against the magic, twisting his neck to keep Ria in view, but he couldn't move.

"I'm going to enjoy killing you!" Ria said, drawing close, and sliding an arm around Tom's neck from behind. Tom gulped, his flesh recoiling from the touch of her knife.

FIZZZZ! Ria let out a startled shriek as she was thrown sideways

by a bolt of energy. She landed hard
on the cobblestones as Tom heard
another magical fizz from somewhere
behind him. Kensa growled with
fury, releasing the energy bolt that
held Tom. He turned to see Daltec

storming towards Kensa, blood
streaming from the cut on his head,
and magical energy crackling around
his hands. Kensa snarled and raised
her own hands, ready to fight. Daltec
let a blue bolt of magic fly just as the
witch fired a sizzling orange dart.

Through the crackle of magic and
the crash of the Beast smashing
the battlements above, Tom heard
a sound that made his blood run
cold. A tiny, joyful giggle. He turned
towards the laughter, and his heart
clenched with horror. Baby Thomas
was toddling across the courtyard,
his little wooden sword in his hand. A
sudden lull in the crashes from above
made Tom look up. *No!* Arkano was
gazing down at Thomas, his yellow

eyes full of malice and deadly smoke puffing from his nostrils.

The Beast clambered down the palace brickwork just as Tom broke into a run, his eyes on the little prince. Baby Thomas turned to look up at the vast, red lizard, and lifted his sword, giggling with delight. Arkano leap from the walls and landed with a thump right in front of the prince. He opened his jaws.

Using the combined powers of his golden boots and golden leg armour, Tom hurtled towards them, knocking benches and glassware flying, quickly nearing Thomas. But as if time had slowed to a crawl, he could see Arkano lowering his head, his eyes narrowing and his huge jaws parting, ready to turn Thomas to stone.

Tom dived towards the child and grabbed him around the chest while covering him with his shield. At the same moment, Arkano let out a grey-black plume of smoke. Snatching

up the prince, Tom leapt aside, just dodging the deadly cloud. He spotted a slender, dark haired figure huddled behind a table. Sara, one of the kitchen maids.

Tom thrust Prince Thomas towards her. "Take him to safety at once!"

As the maid raced away, Tom turned to face the Beast. Arkano prowled towards him, yellow eyes bulging with hate, jaws gaping. Tom tried to lift his shield but realised he couldn't move his arm – or even feel it. He looked down. Cold, grey stone had replaced the flesh of his limb – heavy and dead. His shield, too. His mouth turned dry. He was part statue!

And Arkano was about to finish the job.

5

LURING THE BEAST

Tom sheathed his sword, grabbed the nearest object – a wooden stool – and hurled it at Arkano.

The stool bounced off the creature's brow without leaving a mark. Arkano let out a furious roar, then looked down at Tom, eyes narrowed with rage, and unleashed a jet of smoke. Tom threw himself into a roll, taking cover under a table. As the smoke hit the wood, it crackled and creaked, turning to cold, grey stone.

CRASH! The Beast smashed the table aside with one blow from a mighty forelimb, showering Tom with splinters. Dragging his heavy shield arm, Tom drew his sword and dived between the creature's hind legs, hacking at one as he went. *THWACK!* His blade bit deep into the glowing red flesh, almost severing the leg. Bellowing with pain, Arkano reared away from Tom, eyes rolling madly.

Tom wiped the sweat from his forehead and looked towards Daltec and Kensa, who were still locked in battle. As Kensa aimed a bolt for Daltec, Ria was creeping behind the wizard, knife at the ready. Tom leapt into a clumsy run, but as he tugged his frozen arm behind him, he realised he'd never reach his friend in time. He snatched up a dinner plate, drew back his arm and let it fly.

The plate hit Ria's temple with a thud. She staggered back, clutching her head. Kensa reeled around and thrust both palms in Tom's direction. Every knife laid out for the banquet rose into the air and turned to point his way. Tom gulped as, with another thrust of her hands, Kensa sent them hurtling toward him. He threw himself behind an upturned table, hearing the knives clatter against the wood. Some pierced it, their tips coming within a whisker of his face.

One flew over his head, so close he felt it part his hair.

A booming crash came from the direction of the stables. Tom shot to his feet to see Arkano on the stable roof, ripping at the rafters with his claws.

"Storm!" Tom cried. "Get out of there!" He heard a wild neigh, then the thud of hooves on wood. The stable doors burst open, and Storm cantered out, quickly followed by the other horses. But from the roof, Arkano sent a billowing cloud of smoke over the fleeing steeds. Tom gasped in horror as the two rearmost horses froze, turning to stone mid-stride.

I have to get the Beast out of the City where he can't hurt anyone else.

He put his hand to the red jewel in

his belt. *Arkano! I am Master of the Beasts! Fight me!* The creature's head swivelled around. Arkano's yellow eyes found him. Tom lumbered into a half run, dragging his heavy shield. The Beast reached him before he'd even made it as far as the gatehouse. Tom turned and raised his sword. Arkano let out a hiss, then twisted his reptilian form.

Tom saw the lashing tail too late. *BOOF!* The force of the blow launched Tom towards the gatehouse, his breath punched from his lungs and his sword spinning from his grip. He hit the cobbles beneath the arch and tried to rise, but it hurt too much. Breathless and gasping in agony, he sank back to the ground. The Beast prowled closer, filling Tom's view until all he could see was Arkano's curved teeth dripping with drool.

Through the red jewel, the Beast
spoke.

Now, Master of the Beasts, you die!

6

THE BEAST RISES AGAIN

Elenna raced down the spiral
staircase and emerged in the
courtyard to see the Beast bearing
down on a crumpled figure lying in
the shadow of the gatehouse. *Tom!*
Spying his sword on the flagstones,
she snatched it up. Looking for a
weak spot on the creature's red hide
as she drew close, Elenna noticed

something else – the Beast was standing right under the portcullis. She threw herself towards the pulley and sent Tom's sword flashing downwards with all her strength. *CLANG!* The blade sliced through the chain. Elenna leapt back as the portcullis rattled down.

The iron spikes drove through the glowing flesh of Arkano's back, pinning him to the cobbles. The Beast let out a strangled growl, his body convulsing, froth bubbling from his nostrils. Then all of his yellow eyes fell closed, and he lay still. On the other side of the portcullis, Tom dragged himself to his feet.

"Thanks!" he said, then ducked beneath the lowered spikes of the

portcullis, passing close to the Beast's huge, motionless body.

"One down, two to go!" Elenna said. They both scanned the wreckage of the courtyard. Elenna couldn't see Kensa, but Ria stood before a group of armed guards, sending out crackling zaps of magic to keep them back as they came at her with spears.

Suddenly a hideous metallic grating sound echoed from behind Elenna. She turned to see Arkano heaving himself up, forcing the portcullis higher with his back. "How can he still be alive?" Tom cried as the Beast raised his clawed forelimbs and grabbed the grating, ripping it from its housing. Elenna and Tom dived out of the way as Arkano sent the portcullis flying with a mighty crash.

Tom watched, wide-eyed with disbelief as the Beast limped back into the courtyard, breathing smoke on everything in its path as he lumbered towards Ria.

Elenna suddenly remembered something. "Aduro read a passage in Marlon's diary that described the Beast's fiery heart as his weak spot!"

Tom frowned, nodding slowly. Then he glanced towards the city gates. "I have an idea," he said. "Wait here…" Tom dashed back through the gatehouse.

In the courtyard, the guards were cowering back as the Beast stormed up behind Ria. The young witch let out a wild cackle of laughter. "Afraid of me, are you? Well, you should be!" she said. The guards turned tail and ran. Smiling to herself, Ria turned, then froze. Her eyes widened, and her mouth opened and shut silently as Arkano's shadow fell over her. She turned slowly to face the Beast.

"Nice...er...Beastie?" Ria said, stepping back, her hands raised, palms forwards. "Remember who woke you up, eh? It was me – your good friend, Ria." Elenna fitted an arrow to her bow as Arkano opened his jaws, but even as she let it fly, she knew it would have no effect on the Beast. Ria winced and cowered back as the Beast sent a jet of black smoke towards her. It was no use. The cloud enveloped her and when it cleared,

Elenna saw she was encased, her arms around her head.

The Beast's yellow eyes scanned the courtyard for his next victim. They locked on Elenna.

Her useless bow still raised, Elenna

backed away from the vast monster as he stalked forwards, dragging his injured back leg.

Elenna tried to swallow, but her throat was dry as sand. *Tom, where are you?* she wondered. Arkano opened his massive jaws, showing his long dagger-like teeth. Elenna ducked, waiting to feel the touch of the Beast's deadly breath.

Suddenly, hoofbeats echoed from behind her. She turned to see Storm canter through the gatehouse with Tom on his back. Tom gripped his stallion's sides with just his legs, a lance raised ready in his one good hand, his blue eyes filled with resolve.

Elenna dived out of the stallion's path and Storm swept past her.

Arkano roared with defiance as he spotted Tom hurtling towards him. Tom didn't flinch. Storm didn't break stride. As his stallion sped closer to the Beast, Tom lifted his lance to his shoulder and let it fly. It slammed into the Beast's chest with deadly accuracy, piercing straight through Arkano's body. The Beast's eyes widened with surprise. His mouth opened, letting out a puff of smoke, then he shuddered all over. Finally, the Beast toppled like a tree, sprawling in the ground and lying still. Tom brought Storm around, drawing to a halt beside Elenna and sliding from the saddle.

Her eyes remained on the Beast, expecting him to somehow rise again.

Only this time, he didn't. There was
a strange, crackling sound, coming
from Arkano's body.

"Look," she said, pointing. A thick
black crust was forming over the
Beast's corpse, coating his scales,

almost as if he were being charred by invisible flames. As they watched, the creature's form shrivelled. His eyes sank into their sockets, and his flesh withered away, drying out like an ancient corpse in a tomb, until only a skeleton remained. Then even that fell apart, clattering to the cobbles until there was just a heap of disassembled bones lying in the courtyard.

"We did it!" Tom said, his voice sounding weak with relief. Elenna clapped her friend on the shoulder.

"You did it!" she said. "Ria and Kensa should have known they had no chance against a real Master of the Beasts. And as far as jousting goes – I think you won, fair and square!"

7

A PARTY TO REMEMBER

Tom and Elenna gazed around
the destruction in the courtyard
– scattered food, broken glass,
splintered wood. And dozens of
statues. Despite his victory over
Arkano, Tom felt hollow and sick as
his gaze fell on Captain Harkman,
and the Beast's other victims.

So many lost…

He heard a faint sound. A muffled, protesting voice. "What's that?"

Elenna frowned and pointed to Ria's crouching statue. "It's coming from there."

Together, they wandered closer. And now Tom could see that the stone didn't cover her entirely. In fact, there was a small gap, and he could see a patch of her cheek and a single, angry, swivelling eye.

Hope flared in Tom's chest. *If Ria isn't dead, maybe the other statues aren't, either.* He exchanged a glance with Elenna, and he could see his own hope reflected in her face. Tom lifted his stone arm and smashed it against the ground with all the strength of his magical breastplate.

The stone cracked and fell away, and the feeling returned to Tom's fingers with a fizz of pins and needles.

"I wish I'd tried that earlier!" Tom said, grinning at Elenna. They raced towards Harkman. Tom started

chipping away at the stone encasing the captain with his sword, while Elenna used the tip of an arrow. Daltec emerged from the palace, and quickly came to help them. "Have you seen Kensa?" he asked while he worked. "She ran into the palace, but I lost her."

Tom shook his head. "I'm sure she'll turn up soon enough to help her daughter," he said, gesturing towards Ria. "And when she does, we'll be ready." Working together, the three of them soon uncovered Captain Harkman's eyes, then his mouth and nose. He immediately looked to Arkano's remains .

"You did it?" he said, spitting stone-dust away. "How?"

Tom smiled with joy. "We'll explain

later," he said. "First, we have others to free." Tom left Elenna and Daltec to finish uncovering the captain and headed to the next statue he could find. More people were emerging from the palace now, and Elenna called to them to help with the work. Tom bent over the statue before him and felt a jolt of alarm. It was Sara. The maid he'd left baby Thomas with. His heart hammering, he looked around for a child-sized statue, but there was no sign of the little prince.

"Where's Thomas?" Queen Aroha cried as she rushed from the palace with Hugo right behind her. "He isn't inside! I've checked everywhere!"

"That's because I've got him!" Kensa's sharp voice echoed across the courtyard. Tom turned to see the witch step from the doorway of a tower holding a struggling Prince Thomas in her arms.

"Let him go!" Aroha growled.

"No!" Kensa said, clamping a hand over Thomas's mouth to cut off his piercing scream. "I'm taking him hostage!"

"Then I'll offer you a deal," Aroha said, her eyes desperate as she watched her son struggle in the witch's arms. "My child for yours."

Kensa let out a bark of laughter. "Ria can look after herself!" she said. "I'm off!" She started to chant a spell.

"Mother!" Ria shrieked, her voice muffled by her stone prison. But her cries were drowned out by Kensa's

sudden scream as Thomas sank his
new teeth into her hand. The witch
dropped the child and stumbled
backwards until her legs hit the rim

of Sanek's enormous treasure chest. With a yelp, the witch toppled into the huge, half-empty trunk. Before she could stand, a small figure shot up from his hiding place behind the massive chest, and slammed the lid closed. *Jamil!*

Daltec waved a hand at the chest, zapping the lock with a golden bolt of energy. "That should hold her nicely!" he said. From inside the chest, Tom could hear Kensa's muffled screams.

"Thomas!" Aroha said, scooping the boy into her arms and smothering him with kisses. He still held his small sword, and waved it, smiling happily, ignoring his mother's attention.

King Hugo quickly stepped to the

queen's side. "All's well that ends well. It seems the Beast of the City strikes again, eh?" he said, pinching his son's cheek. Captain Harkman, now free from his stone prison, chuckled too. Even Aroha smiled.

"What shall I do with our two new guests?" Harkman asked Hugo, gesturing to Ria, still imprisoned in stone, and the treasure chest that held Kensa. Loud thumps and muffled cries came from inside.

"Lock them both in the dungeons and throw away the key!" Hugo said.

"I'm having my own cell, then!" Ria snapped, her one visible eye angrier than ever. "You can't expect me to share with her! She was ready to abandon me!"

"I'm sure that can be arranged," Hugo said. "Now, what's to become of the Beast?"

"I think we need to separate the bones, and bury them in different parts of the kingdom," Daltec said. "That way, this can never happen again." Tom looked at the blackened skeleton, and saw Jamil gazing at it too. He felt a sudden rush of sympathy for the boy, all alone, so far from home.

"Jamil," Tom said, approaching the lad. "Thank you for your help capturing Kensa. And I'm guessing you wrote me that note too. I've visited your home, like you told me to, and your parents are both safe. I'll travel back with you, if you like?"

Jamil smiled, and nodded vigorously. "Thank you," he said. "Getting to travel with a real Master of the Beasts would be the best thing ever!"

Tom felt heat rising to his cheeks, but he couldn't help smiling, despite his embarrassment. "It will be an honour to travel with you too!" he said.

"Maybe the treasure that was meant for Sanek can be used to help Jamil's village?" Elenna said.

"Excellent idea, Elenna!" Hugo said, nodding. Then he looked at the devastation all around them, his expression turning grave. "I think we'll all need a bit of time to recover."

Tom took in the broken plates, the scattered food, the chips of stone and splintered timbers. The feast was definitely over before it had even begun.

But this was certainly a birthday party no one will forget in a hurry!

THE END

CONGRATULATIONS, YOU HAVE COMPLETED THIS QUEST!

At the end of each chapter you were
awarded a special gold coin.
The QUEST in this book was
worth an amazing 14 coins.

Look at the Beast Quest totem picture
overleaf to see how far you've come
in your journey to become

MASTER OF THE BEASTS.

The more books you read,
the more coins you will collect!

Do you want your own
Beast Quest Totem?
1. Cut out and collect the coin below
2. Go to the Beast Quest website
3. Download and print out your totem
4. Add your coin to the totem

www.beastquest.co.uk

READ THE BOOKS, COLLECT THE COINS!
EARN COINS FOR EVERY CHAPTER YOU READ!

550+ COINS
MASTER OF
THE BEASTS

410 COINS
HERO →

350 COINS
WARRIOR

230 COINS
KNIGHT →

180 COINS
SQUIRE

44 COINS
PAGE →

550+
515
480
445
410
395
380
365
350
320
290
260
230
217
206
191
180
146
112
78
44
30

31901066644354

← APPRENTICE